Lin-Lin and the Seagulls

Written by Laura Appleton-Smith

Illustrated by Carol Vredenburgh

Laura Appleton-Smith holds a degree in English from Middlebury College. Laura is a primary school teacher who has combined her talents in creative writing with her experience in early childhood education to create *Books to Remember*. She lives in New Hampshire with her husband, Terry.

Carol Vredenburgh graduated Summa Cum Laude from Syracuse University and has worked as an artist and illustrator ever since. This is the fourth book she has illustrated for Flyleaf Publishing.

A Book to Remember™
Published by Flyleaf Publishing

For orders or information, contact us at **(800) 449-7006**.
Please visit our website at **www.flyleafpublishing.com**

First Edition 12/11
Library of Congress Catalog Card Number: 2011941472
ISBN-13: 978-1-60541-134-7
Printed and bound in the USA at Worzalla Publishing, Stevens Point, WI. 12/11

*This story is adapted from an ancient Chinese myth of the Liezi.
The actual myth is printed at the end of this book.*

For Terry

LAS

—

For Isabella, a beautiful free spirit.

CV

Chapter 1

Lin-Lin lived in a hut near the sea.

Lin-Lin loved seagulls.

Each day at sunset, Lin-Lin went to the spot
where the land met the sea.

Standing on the beach in the sunlit swells,
Lin-Lin called to the gulls
and the gulls flocked to her.

If Lin-Lin ran, the seagulls
flapped their wings next to her.

6

If Lin-Lin swam, the seagulls
bobbed on the swells next to her.

8

If Lin-Lin sat on the sand,
the seagulls rested next to her.

As the sun dropped past the tranquil sea,
Lin-Lin was filled with gladness.

Often, on the trip back to her hut,
Lin-Lin stopped to visit the old woman.

The old woman's legs were bent and stiff.
She could not travel to the spot
where the land met the sea.

14

As they drank tea and ate treats,
the old woman asked Lin-Lin to tell her
of the sea
and the gulls
and the sunset.

Lin-Lin was glad to tell the old woman.

Chapter 2

On one visit, the old woman had a basket.

She asked Lin-Lin to bring her six seagulls.

"Lin-Lin, dear, please trap six gulls in this basket.

They can live with me in my hut.

Then I will be happy like you," she said.

On the trip back to her hut, Lin-Lin was distressed. She was very sad.

Lin-Lin wanted the old woman to be happy…

20

But Lin-Lin feared that the spirit of the gulls
would be lost if they lived in a hut and had
no sea,
no sun,
no wind,
and no sand.

Lin-Lin resolved that she must trap the seagulls for the old woman.

It was the least she could do for her.

But still, Lin-Lin was sad.

But when Lin-Lin got to the beach,
to the spot where the land met the sea,
not a gull was there.

And for this,
Lin-Lin was glad!

Folk Tale:

A man who lived by the sea loved seagulls.
Each morning he would go to the seaside and play with the gulls.
Hundreds of gulls would come down and play with him.

His father said, "I understand that seagulls like to play with you.
Catch some seagulls for me so I can play with them, too."

The next morning when the man went to the seaside,
the seagulls would not come down to him.

Liezi

Prerequisite Skills

Single consonants and short vowels
Final double consonants **ff, gg, ll, nn, ss, tt, zz**
Consonant /k/ **ck**
Consonant /j/ **g, dge**
Consonant /s/ **c**
Consonant digraphs /ng/ **ng**, /th/ **th**, /hw/ **wh**
Consonant digraphs /ch/ **ch, tch**, /sh/ **sh**
Schwa /ə/ **a, e, i, o, u**
Long /ā/ **a, a_e**
Long /ē/ **e, e_e, ee, y**
Long /ī/ **i, i_e, igh**
Long /ō/ **o, o_e**
Long /ū/, /o͞o/ **u, u_e**
r-Controlled /ar/ **ar**
r-Controlled /or/ **or**
r-Controlled /ûr/ **er, ir, ur, ear, or**
Variant vowel /aw/ **al, all**
Consonant /l/ **le**
/d/ or /t/ **–ed**

Prerequisite Skills are foundational phonics
skills that have been previously introduced.

Target Letter-Sound Correspondence is
the letter-sound correspondence introduced
in the story.

High-Frequency Puzzle Words are
high-frequency irregular words.

Story Puzzle Words are irregular words
that are not high-frequency.

Decodable Words are words that can be
decoded solely on the basis of the letter-sound
correspondences or phonetic elements that
have been introduced.

Target Letter-Sound Correspondence

Long /ē/ sound spelled **ea**

beach	**please**
dear	sea
each	seagulls
feared	seaside
least	tea
near	treats

Bold indicates high-frequency word.

High-Frequency Puzzle Words

by	said
come	**some**
could	their
day	there
do	they
down	to
father	too
live	wanted
lived	was
loved	were
my	where
of	who
one	would
play	you

Bold indicates new high-frequency word.

Story Puzzle Words

folk tale	woman
often	woman's

Decodable Words

1	catch	**her**	met	**so**	**this**
2	**chapter**	**he**	morning	spirit	tranquil
a	distressed	**him**	**must**	spot	trap
and	drank	**his**	next	standing	travel
as	dropped	hundreds	**no**	stiff	trip
asked	filled	hut	**not**	still	understand
at	flapped	**I**	**old**	stopped	**very**
ate	flocked	**if**	**on**	sun	visit
back	**for**	**in**	past	sunlit	**went**
basket	glad	**it**	ran	sunset	**when**
be	gladness	land	resolved	swam	**will**
bent	**go**	**like**	rested	swells	wind
bobbed	**got**	legs	sad	tell	wings
bring	gull	Lin-Lin	sand	**that**	**with**
but	gulls	lost	sat	**the**	
called	**had**	**man**	**she**	**them**	
can	**happy**	**me**	six	**then**	

Bold indicates high-frequency word.